Staffordshire Library and Information Services
Please return or renew by the last date shown

If not required by other readers, this item may be renewed in person, by post or telephone, online or by email. To renew, either the book or ticket are required

24 Hour Renewal Line
0345 33 00 740

81063/16

Staffordshire
County Council

ECOGRAPHICS

NATURAL RESOURCES

Izzi Howell

W

FRANKLIN WATTS

LONDON • SYDNEY

Franklin Watts

First published in Great Britain in 2019 by The Watts Publishing Group

Copyright © The Watts Publishing Group 2019

 Produced for Franklin Watts by
White-Thomson Publishing Ltd
www.wtpub.co.uk
01273 479982

Editor: Izzi Howell
Designer: Clare Nicholas
Cover designer: Steve Mead

Alamy: Planetpix 11b; Getty: Stockbyte 11t, Kiyoshi Ota/Bloomberg 19, ALBERT GONZALEZ FARRAN/AFP 23, simonkr 26; Shutterstock: hxdbzxy 5, Roel Slootweg 7, Wisit Tongma 8, Kletr 12, Dr Morley Read 15, salajean 17, DJTaylor 21, MicheleB 22, Marcio Jose Bastos Silva 24, Rido 29.

All design elements from Shutterstock.

ISBN 978 1 4451 6598 1

Printed in Dubai

 MIX
Paper from
responsible sources
FSC® C104740
FSC
www.fsc.org

Franklin Watts
An imprint of
Hachette Children's Group
Part of The Watts Publishing Group
Carmelite House
50 Victoria Embankment
London EC4Y 0DZ

An Hachette UK Company
www.hachette.co.uk
www.franklinwatts.co.uk

Contents

What are natural resources?

Natural resources are things we use that come from nature, such as wood, metal and water. We use these resources for construction, food and technology, as well as to produce energy and power vehicles.

Renewable resources

Natural resources can be renewable or non-renewable. The supply of renewable resources will never run out. The amount of these resources, which include sunlight, water and wind, always stays the same. Some natural resources, such as plants and crops for food, can be regrown. As long as we continue to plant these resources, our supply will not run out.

Natural resources on Earth include ...

coal
(see pages 8–9)

metal and stone
(see pages 16–17)

wood
(see pages 12–13)

oil
(see pages 8–9)

Non-renewable resources

Other natural resources are non-renewable, such as natural gas, oil, coal and certain minerals. We have a limited amount of these resources, as it takes millions of years for them to form. At the moment, we are not using these resources in a sustainable way. If we continue to use them at current rates, our supply will eventually run out.

We use a huge amount of petrol (a form of oil) as fuel for vehicles such as cars, planes and lorries.

Consequences

Using some resources has a negative impact on the environment. Burning fossil fuels, such as coal, oil and natural gas, causes the temperature on Earth to rise (see page 9). Cutting down trees for timber and clearing forests for farmland destroys ecosystems and affects plant and animal life.

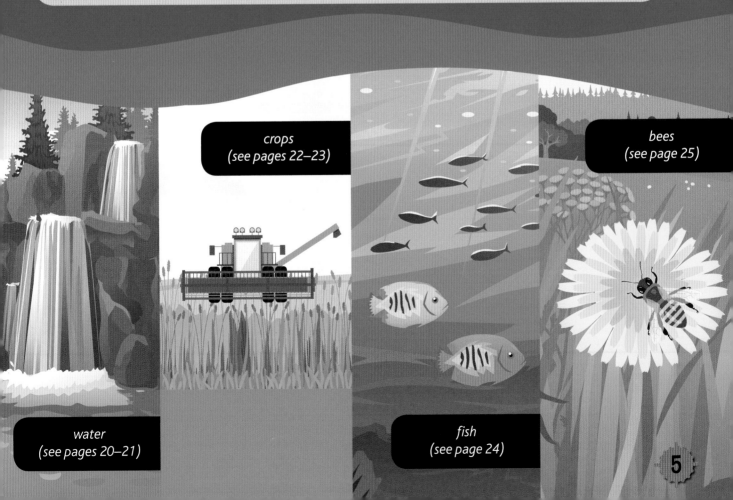

crops
(see pages 22–23)

bees
(see page 25)

water
(see pages 20–21)

fish
(see page 24)

Resource distribution

Some areas around the world have more natural resources than others. The amount of resources used by people is different in every country.

Raw materials

Many resources come from less economically developed countries. They supply raw materials such as metals, timber and some crops. Some of these resources are processed into items such as cars, mobile phones or furniture.

Trade

Trade allows countries to get resources that they need that are not available in their country. However, trade depends on the wealth of the country. Not every country can buy all the resources that its citizens need.

Using resources

The amount of resources used in different countries varies a lot. People in more economically developed countries consume far more resources than people in less economically developed countries. They own more objects, drive large cars and live in bigger houses that require more energy to run.

Average quantity of resources used every day per person in North America and Africa:

90 kg North America

10 kg Africa

Environmental damage

Less economically developed countries can grow economically and become more developed by selling their resources. However, extracting these resources can have a serious impact on the environment in these countries. Drilling for oil, pesticides used in farming and mining can all damage the land and kill wild animals and plants. Deforestation can in turn lead to desertification, where the land turns into a desert.

This lake in Madagascar has been polluted and turned red by waste from a mine.

Population size

The use of resources is linked to population size. As the global population increases, so will the demand for resources. There are already 7.6 billion people on Earth, but this number may rise to over 9 billion by 2050. The Earth may not contain enough resources to support such a high population, especially if people use excessive quantities of resources, for example by living in very large houses that require a lot of energy to run.

We currently extract **60** billion tonnes of resources every year. By 2030, we may need to extract **100** billion tonnes to support the world population.

Oil, gas and coal

Oil, natural gas and coal are valuable resources that are burned as fuel and used to generate electricity. They are non-renewable resources, and there is a real risk that they may run out within the next 100 years.

Fossil fuels

Oil, natural gas and coal are known as fossil fuels. They formed over millions of years from the remains of dead plants and animals. They are found underground.

Drilling for oil and natural gas

To access oil and natural gas, workers drill holes deep in the ground. They use pumps to draw the resources up to the surface. Reserves of oil and natural gas are often found in the rock underneath the sea bed.

Oil platforms are structures built at sea, with equipment to drill and store oil and natural gas. Ships carry the oil and natural gas to shore.

Creating electricity

Oil, coal and natural gas are burned in power plants to generate heat. When they are burned, they create heat, which is used to boil water. The boiling water makes steam, which makes a turbine spin. The spinning turbine powers a generator, which produces electricity.

Coal mines

Most coal is dug out of the Earth in mines deep underground. In some areas, the entire top of a mountain is removed to access the coal inside.

The end of fossil fuels

Our supply of fossil fuels is running low. We have the smallest reserve of oil, followed by natural gas and coal.

2052

Oil – We are currently using 11 billion tonnes a year. If this continues, we will have run out by around 2052.

2060

Natural gas – Use of natural gas will probably increase after our oil supplies run out. Due to this increase, supplies of natural gas will run out in around 2060.

2088

Coal – After natural gas and oil run out, use of coal will probably increase as well. Because of this, supplies will probably only last until around 2088.

Fracking

Fracking is a method of extracting natural gas and oil that are trapped inside shale rock. Water, sand and chemicals are injected into the rock to break it apart so that the natural gas and oil are released. As supplies of fossil fuels run low, fracking is one way of accessing more resources. However, the process is controversial. It damages the environment through its heavy use of water and poisonous chemicals, and it may even cause small earthquakes.

The greenhouse effect

When fossil fuels are burned, they release carbon dioxide. This gas gathers in the atmosphere around the Earth. It traps heat energy from the Sun's light, which increases the temperature on Earth and leads to climate change. This is known as the greenhouse effect.

Arctic oil

As oil begins to run out in some areas, oil companies are starting to look for new places to drill. The Arctic sea bed is one site where oil and natural gas could be extracted, but at great risk to the environment.

Up to **160** billion barrels of oil could lie under the Arctic sea bed.

Why now?

In the past, oil companies didn't have the technology to extract oil from under the deep Arctic sea bed. New equipment and technology will make this process simpler and safer. Blocks of sheet ice that previously covered the Arctic Ocean are now melting because of climate change. This makes it easier for ships to reach these areas.

More oil

Some people are concerned about drilling for oil in the Arctic because they don't think that we should be extracting more oil to be used as fuel. Burning this oil will contribute to further climate change. Many scientists think it's better to leave any remaining oil in the ground and instead invest in alternative sources of energy that are less damaging to the environment (see page 28).

Threats

Drilling for oil in the Arctic will also damage fragile ecosystems. Chemicals used in drilling will poison the water, affecting fish and other animals that depend on fish for food. Loud drilling noises will travel through the water, disturbing animals that use sound to navigate, such as dolphins and whales.

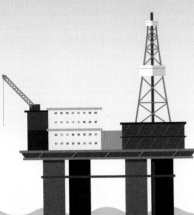

Oil spills

Icebergs and stormy weather in the Arctic Ocean will make it difficult for ships to carry oil to shore. Oil spills are likely to happen. When oil gets into the ocean, it covers sea birds' feathers and sea mammals' fur. This makes it harder for them to keep warm and float in the water. When the animals try to clean themselves, the oil can get inside their bodies and poison them.

There is a
75% chance
of a major oil spill
if Arctic oil is
extracted.

An environmental charity organises a protest against Arctic oil drilling in Washington DC, USA. Charities are trying to create new protected areas in the Arctic to help save the animals that live there.

Fighting back

Environmental charities are trying to stop drilling for Arctic oil by taking countries to court. They believe that plans to drill for more oil mean that the countries are breaking climate change agreements. In the meantime, scientists are trying to develop new oil-drilling methods and transport systems that are less likely to spill and damage the Arctic environment.

Wood

Wood is a renewable resource. If our supply of wood is managed properly, it will not run out. However, in some areas wood is being gathered in an unsustainable way. Chopping down trees is also damaging some ecosystems.

Uses

Wood is used in many ways. It is a building material for houses, furniture and other structures. It can also be processed to make paper and cardboard. In less developed countries in particular, wood is often burned as a fuel, as people do not have access to electric heating and stoves.

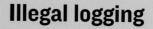

Logging

The process of cutting down trees is called logging. Loggers use huge, powerful saws to cut through the trunk of a tree. The trunks are then sent to sawmills, where they are cut into smaller pieces of wood. Most countries have rules about the quantity and type of trees loggers can cut down. This protects woodland and rainforest ecosystems.

Loggers use mechanical arms to pick up the heavy logs. They transport them to the sawmill by truck.

Illegal logging

In some countries, such as Russia, Brazil and Indonesia, loggers work illegally. They cut down too many trees, or gather wood from protected areas or endangered trees. This reduces biodiversity in woodlands and rainforests, as these trees provide food and shelter to plants and animals. It also takes money away from local communities who operate legally and depend on legal logging for their income.

Sustainable logging

Sustainable logging is one way of producing timber while still protecting the environment. Instead of cutting down wild trees, farmers plant huge amounts of the same type of fast-growing tree on a tree plantation. These trees are cut down when they are ready and more trees are planted in their place. This secures the supply of wood for the future.

Deforestation

Not all trees are cut down to be used for their wood. In some regions, such as Southeast Asia and Brazil, large areas of rainforest are cut down so that the land can be used for farming or construction. This is known as deforestation.

Half of the world's rainforest has been cut down or cleared in the last 100 years.

Forest fires

Forest fires are a natural threat to our wood supply. They are sometimes started when lightning hits dry plants, and sets them alight. The fire then spreads rapidly through the nearby area, destroying any trees and plants in its path. Forest fires are becoming more common because of global warming. Human activity can also start forest fires.

Reforestation

Rainforests and woodlands can be brought back to life by planting new trees. This is called reforestation. However, it has to be done carefully or the ecosystem will not recover properly.

Around the world

Many countries are starting to realise the importance of forests. They are planning large-scale reforestation to recover the trees that have been destroyed through logging or land clearance.

Planned reforestation (in million hectares)

13 India

20 South America

over 100 Africa

Tree plantations

Not all replantation is good for biodiversity, however. A tree plantation, where just one type of fast-growing tree is planted, is a sustainable way of producing wood and protecting wild forests (see page 13). However, these trees may not provide the right food or shelter for animals that previously lived in the habitat.

Recovering biodiversity

To create new, biodiverse forest habitats, different species of trees need to be planted. Each species provides food and shelter for different animals. It's also important to plant native trees. Introduced trees may disturb the balance of the ecosystem and affect the growth of native trees by blocking their light or absorbing too much water from the ground.

Some animals live high in the branches of tall trees, while others live in low trees, closer to the ground.

Difficulties

Reforestation needs to be carefully managed. Newly planted trees require a great deal of water while they are growing. Some trees may need to be watered, as there isn't enough rain to keep them alive. Looking after new trees is expensive. Many less economically developed countries, which suffer the most from deforestation to begin with, cannot afford the costs.

Agroforestry

In agroforestry, crops are planted around wild forests, allowing both plants to grow together. This is a good solution to deforestation for less economically developed countries. The trees' leaves provide shade for the crops and protect them from heavy rain.

In this agroforestry farm in Ecuador, coffee plants are grown among native rainforest trees.

Metal and stone

Metal and stone are dug out of the Earth. They are used for construction, technology and to make jewellery.

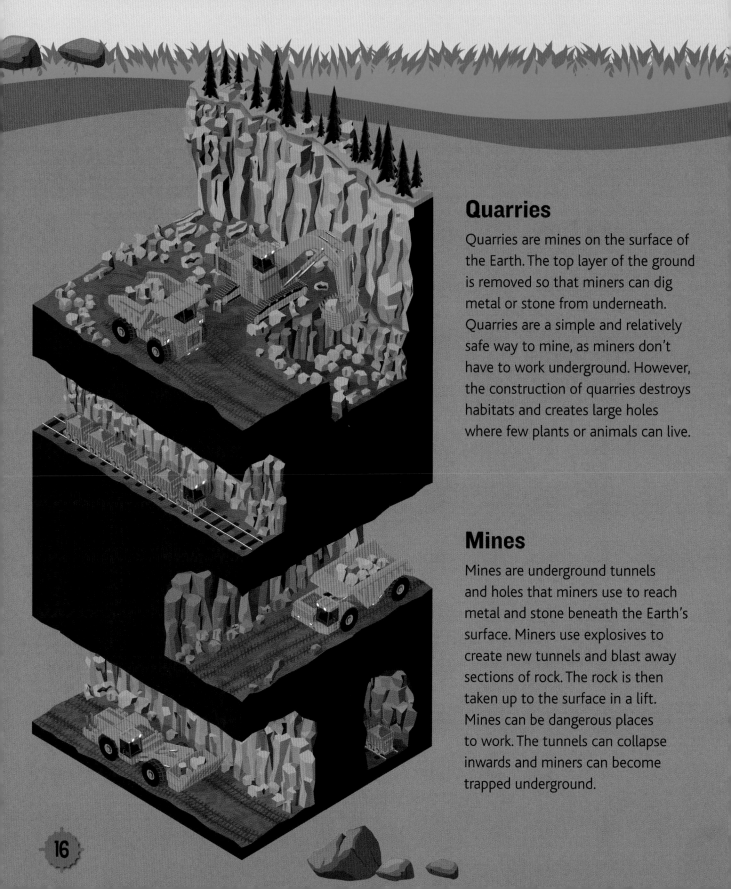

Quarries

Quarries are mines on the surface of the Earth. The top layer of the ground is removed so that miners can dig metal or stone from underneath. Quarries are a simple and relatively safe way to mine, as miners don't have to work underground. However, the construction of quarries destroys habitats and creates large holes where few plants or animals can live.

Mines

Mines are underground tunnels and holes that miners use to reach metal and stone beneath the Earth's surface. Miners use explosives to create new tunnels and blast away sections of rock. The rock is then taken up to the surface in a lift. Mines can be dangerous places to work. The tunnels can collapse inwards and miners can become trapped underground.

Rock to metal

Most metals do not exist in a pure state in the ground. They are found as an ore – a mixture of metal and other minerals. For example, aluminium is nearly always found as bauxite ore, rather than as pure aluminium. Metal ore is heated until the metal melts and can be separated from the other minerals.

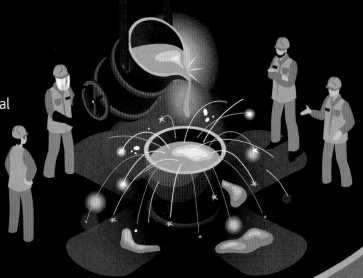

Supply

Metal and stone are non-renewable resources. However, there is still a large amount of these resources left in the ground, so we are not at risk of running out soon.

The water in this lake in Romania has been turned red because of iron pollution from mining.

Environmental impact

Mining metal and stone has a negative impact on the environment. Chemicals used in mining and waste are washed onto nearby land, polluting it and harming the plants and animals that live there. The machines used to drill into the ground and transport metal and stone also run on fossil fuels, which contribute to the greenhouse effect.

Reuse and recycle

To avoid further environmental damage caused by mining, it is much better for us to reuse and recycle the stone and metal that we have already gathered, rather than collecting more. This will also help us to preserve our supply of these resources for longer.

Rare earth metals

Rare earth metals are a group of seventeen metals that are used in almost every kind of modern technology, from headphones to wind turbines. These metals are hard to find, which is why they are called 'rare'. Some rare earth metals and their products include ...

YTTRIUM
TV and computer screens, energy-efficient light bulbs

GADOLINIUM
nuclear reactor shields, X-ray machines

LANTHANUM
camera and telescope lenses

NEODYMIUM
loudspeakers, wind turbines

Sources

There are actually large amounts of rare earth metals in the Earth's crust. However, these metals are spread out over a huge area and it is unusual to find many in one place. They are nearly always found mixed with other minerals in ores. For this reason, sourcing rare earth metals is a slow and difficult process.

Location

Around 90 per cent of the world's supply of rare earth metals comes from mines in China. This is a potential problem, as it means that China could stop other countries from making technology by cutting off their supply of rare earth metals or by raising the prices too high. Other areas are currently being surveyed for rare earth minerals, including Japan, the USA and Brazil.

Scientists believe that they have found a source of **14.5 million tonnes** of rare earth metals in the sea bed off the coast of Japan.

Demand and supply

At the moment, the demand for rare earth metals is greater than its supply. This is due to the explosion in new technology that has taken place over the the past twenty years. As new types of technology are developed, and demand continues to grow, we may face a shortage of rare earth metals in the future.

Recycling

Some of the rare earth metals in pieces of technology can be recycled. This helps to reduce the demand for new mined metals and stops these metals from being wasted in landfill. However, only small amounts of rare earth metals are used in devices such as mobile phones, so it is very difficult to extract them and recycle them.

Water

Water is a very important resource. It isn't just used for drinking. It's also needed for industry, agriculture and household use, such as washing machines.

Only **2.5%** of water on Earth is fresh water.

Water on Earth

Almost all of the water on Earth is salt water, found in the oceans. There is only a very small amount of the fresh water that humans need for most tasks. This makes it a rare and valuable resource.

Finding water

Fresh water is found in lakes and rivers. It can also be pumped up from below the ground. In some dry areas with few lakes or rivers, salt is removed from sea water so that the water can be used for drinking and cleaning. However, this process is very expensive and consumes a lot of electricity.

Using water

More economically developed countries use much more water than less economically developed countries. This is because people in more economically developed countries tend to own objects that use a great deal of water, such as dishwashers.

Industry and agriculture

Most of the water consumed by less economically developed countries is used in industry and agriculture. Water is used in fossil-fuel power stations to generate electricity (see page 8), which is used to power factories. Raising animals to eat for food also uses water, which is needed for the animals to drink and for growing food for them to eat, such as hay.

The amount of water needed to produce 1 kg of food

beef – 15,415 litres
chicken – 4,325 litres
rice – 2,497 litres
bread – 1,608 litres
apples – 822 litres
potatoes – 287 litres

Clean water

Water in lakes and rivers can contain bacteria that can make people sick. These bacteria can come from human waste or pollution. Water is treated to kill the bacteria before it travels through pipes into people's homes.

Around the world

Many people do not have a reliable water supply. They have no water pipes in their homes or villages. They have to walk long distances to gather water from wells and carry it back to their homes. Sometimes, they have no choice other than to use untreated water from lakes and rivers.

Using less water

Fresh water is a valuable resource that we must not waste. Factories can recycle the water that they use, rather than using new water. At home, people could use water from baths or showers to water their plants.

This woman has collected rain water in a water butt, which she is using to water her plants.

One small step

Turn off the tap while brushing your teeth. A running tap uses 6 litres of water per minute.

Farming

Farmers grow crops and raise animals to provide people with food. Some people worry that climate change and the world's growing population may make it harder for us to produce enough food in the future.

Crops

Fruit, vegetables and grains are crops grown by farmers. They need fertile soil and water to grow. They are very important to our food supply. Grains, such as rice and wheat, provide the main part of most people's diets around the world.

A farmer in China harvests a field of rice.

Rice provides over one fifth of all calories eaten around the world.

Problems

There are many issues that threaten our food supply. Very high temperatures and drought, caused by global warming, can kill crops before they are ready to eat. Cleared forest land is often not very fertile. It can be hard for farmers to grow crops on it. Crops are also at risk because of the decline of bee populations (see page 25).

Import and export

Many crops are grown in less economically developed countries. They are often exported to more economically developed countries to be eaten. Transporting food around the world creates pollution and greenhouse gases.

One small step

Try to use up every bit of food that you buy. Save leftover food from dinner for lunch the next day.

Hunger and famine

Many people around the world do not have a secure food supply. This isn't because there is not enough food to go round, but because of poverty. People in less economically developed countries may not earn enough money to buy food, so they go hungry. When crops fail, countries often do not have enough money to import food for their citizens. This can lead to famine and death.

Women in South Sudan share out donated corn in 2017. South Sudan has been seriously affected by drought and famine, despite food aid from other countries.

GM crops

Scientists have created genetically modified (GM) crops that are more resistant to high temperatures and poor growing conditions. They also produce more food. Some people believe that GM crops will help us to protect our food supply. Others worry that there may be long-term problems with eating GM crops, as there hasn't been much research done yet.

Wildlife

Wild plants and animals are an important resource. Some species, such as fish, are a source of food. Others carry out important roles that help us to survive.

Fish

Fish are one of the few wild animals that we eat in large numbers. We also eat some fish that are raised on farms. Our supply of fish has been affected by fishermen catching too many of them, especially young fish. They don't leave enough fish to reproduce, so the population can't recover. Rules that control the size and number of fish that fisherman can catch have helped fish populations to grow again.

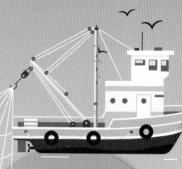

The number of cod in the North Sea has multiplied by **4** since 2006!

Plants

During photosynthesis (the process by which plants produce energy), plants release oxygen. Humans breathe in this oxygen, which the human body needs to work properly. Without plants on Earth, there would not be enough oxygen for humans to survive.

Pollination

Animals such as bees and butterflies help to pollinate (fertilise) wild plants. When they land on flowers to drink nectar, pollen sticks to their legs. They carry this pollen to every flower that they visit, fertilising the other flowers. Without pollination, plants would not produce seeds for new plants. We would lose our supply of strawberries, cotton and potatoes, among others.

Around 70 per cent of the oxygen in the atmosphere is produced by marine plants, such as kelp and plankton.

Carbon dioxide →

← Oxygen

FOCUS ON Bees

Bees play an important role in the pollination of plants. However, some species of bee are dying out. Our food supply will be seriously affected if bees continue to disappear.

Why?

Different species of bee are declining for different reasons.

Pesticides

Some pesticides used to kill insects that destroy crops also harm bees. They damage the bees' ability to navigate, reproduce and fly.

Habitat loss

The wildflower meadows where some bees feed on nectar and pollen are being destroyed and turned into farmland.

Climate change

Flowers are blooming earlier in the year because of global warming. Some bees don't come out of their hive until later, when the flowers used to bloom. They miss the opportunity for food and so they starve.

Diseases

Recent outbreaks of bee diseases have affected some species around the world.

Solutions

There are several ways in which we can help to protect bees. The EU has already banned some pesticides that harm bees. Protecting and replanting wildflower areas will create new sources of food for hungry bees.

One small step

Plant flowering plants that bees like to visit, such as lavender, ivy and apple trees, in the school playground or at home.

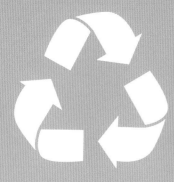

Recycling

Recycling is a great way of using fewer resources.
It also cuts down on pollution and energy use.

Things to recycle

Many items can be recycled.
In most areas, paper, cardboard,
plastic, glass, metal and textiles
can be recycled. In many places,
recycling is collected from
people's houses.

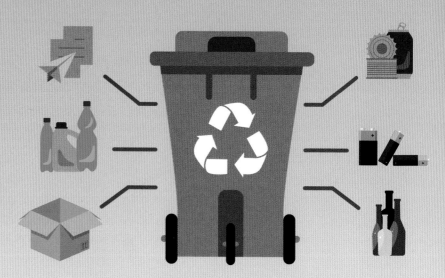

Recycling materials
uses **95% less**
energy than making
new materials
from scratch.

*Workers at a
recycling plant
sort paper on a
conveyor belt.*

Recycling problems

Recycling does consume some resources. Plastic is used
to make recycling containers and bins. Fuel is needed to
power recycling collection vehicles and the machines at
recycling plants.

One small step

Try a paper recycling challenge
at home or at school for one
week. Every unwanted piece
of paper must be recycled –
nothing can go in the bin!

Reduce and reuse

Reusing objects and reducing the amount you consume is even better for the environment than recycling. This is because no new resources or energy are needed, unlike recycling. If everyone reduced or reused a few objects, it would make a big difference. Try using reusable water bottles and shopping bags, and getting clothes and other items from charity shops rather than buying them new.

Landfill

If objects aren't reused or recycled, they are often sent to landfill sites when they are thrown away. Landfill sites are holes in the ground where rubbish is stored. Glass, plastic and metal can take millions of years to break down, so these objects will stay in the soil for a long time. Landfill sites pollute the ground around them, so the land can't be lived on or used for agriculture. They also create greenhouse gases, such as methane, which contribute to global warming.

Burning waste

In some places, rubbish is burned in incinerators. This reduces the amount of waste sent to landfill. However, burning waste releases greenhouse gases and toxic gases that can cause breathing problems and other health issues for people who live nearby.

Food waste

We can't recycle food, but we can make compost from food waste, such as leftover bread and meat, fruit and vegetable peelings, and egg shells. In the right conditions, this waste quickly breaks down and becomes compost. Compost can be added to soil to fertilise it, so that crops can grow better.

Managing natural resources

It's important to manage the remaining natural resources on Earth. This will save them for future generations to use and help to preserve the environment.

Renewable energy

More and more countries are working on changing from non-renewable to renewable sources of energy, such as solar, wind and hydroelectric power, and geothermal energy (heat from the Earth). Using renewable forms of energy will reduce the use of fossil fuels and prevent further climate change.

wind energy

solar energy

hydroelectric dam

geothermal energy

The age of electricity

Some car manufacturers are now producing cars that run partly or entirely on electricity, rather than petrol made from oil. Driving an electric car uses fewer resources. If the electricity used to power the car comes from renewable sources, electric cars are a very sustainable form of transport. Vehicles that run on biofuel (fuel that comes from plants) are also becoming increasingly popular.

A recovering world

It's not too late to undo damage that has been done to the planet through overuse of resources. We can replant trees sustainably (see page 15) and help plant and animal life to return. By following rules about sustainable fishing and pesticide use, fish and insect populations should eventually be restored.

Organic fruit and vegetables are grown without pesticides that harm insects. By eating organic food where possible, we can help protect insects such as bees.

One small step

Talk to your friends and family about using natural resources responsibly. Share some of the ideas in this book with them.

Doing our part

Industries and governments have the most responsibility for managing resources wisely. However, we can all help. Try to use less water at home and at school. Reduce, reuse and recycle as much as you can. See if your school can install solar panels to produce some of the electricity it uses.

Glossary

atmosphere the layer of gases around the Earth

climate change changes to the weather on Earth

crops plants that are grown in large amounts

deforestation cutting down trees and clearing land

demand a need for something to be supplied or sold

desertification when fertile land turns into a desert

drought a period when there isn't enough water

ecosystem all the living things in an area

extract to take something out

famine a long period of time when people in an area do not have enough food

fossil fuel a fuel that comes from the ground, such as coal, oil or natural gas

geothermal related to heat from inside the Earth

global warming an increase in the temperature around the world because of the greenhouse effect

greenhouse gas a gas that traps heat in the atmosphere, such as carbon dioxide

native something that grows or lives naturally in a place and has not been brought from somewhere else

non-renewable describes something that can't be reproduced and can run out

ore a mixture of metal and other minerals

pesticide a chemical used to kill insects and other living things that harm plants

pollinate to fertilise a plant

raw a raw resource has not been processed

renewable describes something that can be reproduced and will not run out

reserve the amount of something that is left

resistant not harmed or affected by something

sustainable describes something that can continue for a long time because it does not harm the environment

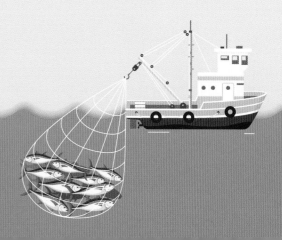

Further reading

Energy and Fuel (Get the Whole Picture) by Paul Mason (Wayland, 2019)

Geographics: Earth's Resources by Izzi Howell (Franklin Watts, 2018)

EcoSTEAM: The Stuff We Buy by Georgia Amson-Bradshaw (Wayland, 2018)

Websites

climatekids.nasa.gov/recycle-this/
Play a recycling game and learn recycling facts.

www.theworldcounts.com
See in real time how resources are used.

www.bbc.co.uk/guides/ztxwqty
Find out more about renewable and non-renewable sources of energy.

www.epa.gov/watersense/watersense-kids
Learn simple ways to save water.

Note to parents and teachers:
Every effort has been made by the publisher to ensure that these websites contain no inappropriate or offensive material. However, because of the nature of the Internet, it is impossible to guarantee that the content of these sites will not be altered. We strongly advise that Internet access is supervised by a responsible adult.

Index

ECOGRAPHICS

Series contents lists

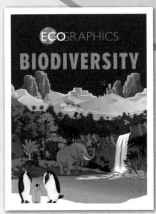

BIODIVERSITY

HB: 978 1 4451 6596 7
PB: 978 1 4451 6597 4

● What is biodiversity? ● Genetic diversity ● Ecosystems ● Focus on keystone species ● Deforestation ● Focus on the Amazon Rainforest ● Climate change ● Pollution ● Hunting ● Focus on the ivory trade ● Invasive species ● Consequences ● Back from the brink ● Focus on the bald eagle ● Focus on the humpback whale

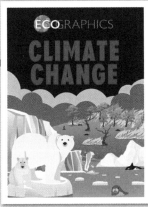

CLIMATE CHANGE

HB: 978 1 4451 6571 4
PB: 978 1 4451 6572 1

● What is climate change? ● Fossil fuels ● Global warming ● Rising sea levels ● Focus on the Greenland ice sheet ● Farming and food ● Habitats and wildlife ● Focus on sea turtles ● Desertification ● Focus on desertification in China ● Extreme weather ● Focus on Hurricane Harvey ● Stopping climate change

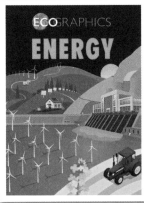

ENERGY

HB: 978 1 4451 6644 5
PB: 978 1 4451 6645 2

● What is energy? ● Fossil fuels ● Focus on natural gas ● Nuclear power ● Solar power ● Focus on California ● Hydroelectric power ● Focus on the Itaipu Dam ● Biomass ● Wind power ● Geothermal energy ● Focus on Iceland ● The future of energy

NATURAL RESOURCES

HB: 978 1 4451 6598 1
PB: 978 1 4451 6599 8

● What are natural resources? ● Resource distribution ● Oil, gas and coal ● Focus on Arctic oil ● Wood ● Focus on reforestation ● Metal and stone ● Focus on rare earth metals ● Water ● Farming ● Wildlife ● Focus on bees ● Recycling ● Managing natural resources

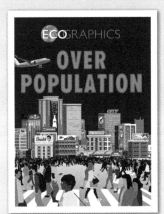

OVER POPULATION

HB: 978 1 4451 6642 1
PB: 978 1 4451 6643 8

● What is overpopulation? ● Distribution and density ● Focus on Singapore ● Births and deaths ● Focus on Niger and Russia ● Migration ● Focus on Syria ● Resources ● Focus on drought-resistant crops ● Water ● Cities ● Focus on Mumbai ● Solutions

POLLUTION

HB: 978 1 4451 6600 1
PB: 978 1 4451 6601 8

● What is pollution? ● Water ● Focus on Lake Erie ● Ocean plastic ● Focus on the Great Pacific Garbage Patch ● Landfills ● Air ● The greenhouse effect ● Focus on air pollution in India ● Nuclear waste ● Focus on Fukushima ● Light and sound ● Reducing pollution

FRANKLIN WATTS